PUFFIN BOOKS

Published by the Penguin Group
Penguin Books Ltd, 80 Strand, London WC2R 0RL, England
Penguin Group (USA) Inc., 375 Hudson Street, New York, New York 10014, USA
Penguin Group (Canada), 90 Eglinton Avenue East, Suite 700, Toronto, Ontario, Canada M4P 2Y3
(a division of Pearson Penguin Canada Inc.)
Penguin Ireland, 25 St Stephen's Green, Dublin 2, Ireland (a division of Penguin Books Ltd)
Penguin Group (Australia), 250 Camberwell Road, Camberwell, Victoria 3124, Australia
(a division of Pearson Australia Group Pty Ltd)
Penguin Books India Pvt Ltd, 11 Community Centre, Panchsheel Park, New Delhi – 110 017, India
Penguin Group (NZ), 67 Apollo Drive, Mairangi Bay, Auckland 1310, New Zealand
(a division of Pearson New Zealand Ltd)
Penguin Books (South Africa) (Pty) Ltd, 24 Sturdee Avenue, Rosebank, Johannesburg 2196, South Africa

Penguin Books Ltd, Registered Offices: 80 Strand, London WC2R 0RL, England

penguin.com

First published in the USA by HarperCollins 2007
First published in Great Britain by Puffin Books 2007
1 3 5 7 9 10 8 6 4 2

Made and printed in Trento, Italy

British Library Cataloguing in Publication Data
A CIP catalogue record for this book is available from the British Library

ISBN: 978–0–141–32145–5

Charlotte's Web

New in the Barn

Adapted by Catherine Hapka
Based on the Motion Picture Screenplay by
Susanna Grant & Karey Kirkpatrick
Based on the book by E. B. White

PUFFIN

Fern Arable watched in wonder as eleven piglets were born. One of them was smaller than the others. "That's the runt of the litter," Fern's father said.

"I'll feed you and care for you," Fern promised the tiny pig.

She decided to name him Wilbur.

From that day on, Fern and Wilbur were inseparable. He slept in bed with her, went to school with her, and took long walks with her.

But baby pigs grow quickly. Wilbur was getting big.
He couldn't help being in the way.
Finally Fern's father made a decision.
"I'm sorry, Fern," he said. "But it's time for the pig to go."

Fern couldn't believe her ears.
How could her father send away her best friend?
"I promised to take care of him!"
she protested.
"I'm letting you out of your promise,"
her father replied.
"I didn't promise *you*," Fern cried.
"I promised Wilbur!"

Fern was still upset the next day.

"What about Homer?" Fern's mother suggested. "I'm sure he could make room for a pig."

"Uncle Homer?" Fern said.

That didn't sound too bad. Homer Zuckerman's farm was right next door. Maybe Wilbur would be OK there . . .

Zuckerman's barn looked big and scary.

"You'll be OK," Fern told Wilbur sadly. "You'll make lots of new friends here."

Wilbur was frightened. He was used to going everywhere with Fern. He didn't want to be left behind!

He squealed and tried to follow Fern. "I'll come see you every day," Fern said, as she closed the gate behind her. A tear fell from her cheek.

Then . . . she was gone.

SQUEEEEE!

Wilbur squealed in terror again and again. He threw himself against the fence, trying to break free. But the fence was strong. It didn't budge.

The other animals woke up and looked to see what was causing all the racket.

The sheep watched Wilbur. Golly and Gussy the geese watched, too.

Wilbur didn't pay any attention. He was still busy ramming the fence.

Snap!

Finally a fence board broke.

"Pig's out!" Golly cried, as Wilbur raced up the lane.

"Since when do we have a pig?" Ike asked, confused.

Mr Zuckerman and his farmhand ran to catch Wilbur.

Wilbur saw them coming and ran away. The other animals cheered as they watched.

But suddenly Wilbur stopped and smiled. He smelled something familiar . . . something delicious . . . slops!

"Here, piggy piggy," Mr Zuckerman said, holding a pail.

Eating the slops made Wilbur feel better. "I'm better off here in the barn," he said. "I'm much too young to be out there alone."

The other animals watched him eat. Wilbur hoped they would soon be his friends – the sheep, the horse, the geese and all the rest.

Fern was right. Things would be OK.

As Wilbur lay down for his night's sleep, he didn't notice one more creature watching him from a dark corner of the barn – a spider.

Little did he know that soon, the tiny grey spider would become his very special friend, Charlotte.